I0545692

The Woman In Apartment 3D

A "Holy Rock Chronicles" Story

SCANLIFE

Get more Info About Shelia E. Bell books!

The Woman In Apartment 3D
A "Holy Rock Chronicles" Story

Get more Info About Shelia E. Bell books!

NATIONAL BESTSELLING AUTHOR

SHELIA E. BELL

Holy Rock Chronicles
is a series of three (3) short stories featuring members of the infamous Holy Rock Ministries (*My Son's Wife* series). *The Woman in Apartment 3D* is story #2. These three short stories will be released every 60 days. They are meant to give you a behind the scenes peek at what some of the characters are doing while I'm busy writing *Thicker Than Water* installment #11 of the *My Son's Wife* series! (smile) Scheduled for release July 20th! I hope you enjoy this second one. Thanks as always for choosing to read my work!

Books 1-3
Calling Dr. Daniels
The Woman in Apartment 3D
Ruthless Rianna

Acknowledgements

To all those who have supported my career and continue to support me over the years—thank you. To those who have just taken their first chance on reading my literary work—thank you! I'm fortunate and blessed to do something I absolutely love. When I am weaving and creating stories, I feel like I am living my very own purpose driven life.

Thank you to every book club, every avid reader, every book promoter, and every person who is in the literary arena. An extra special thanks to Rolonda (Frazier) Bridgewater! Rolonda, thank you for your invaluable advice, for being an avid reader of my work, and being one of my top literary supporters.

Extra special thanks to my three sons—I love you and I appreciate you for sticking by me, helping me, loving me, caring for me, and being the best sons a mom could ever have!

Always thanks to my mommy for supporting me in all my endeavors and for singing my praises to whoever will listen. I love you, Mommy.

A very extra special "Thank you" to Ethel Woodard, *aka author Eve Alexander*, for sharing your vast literary knowledge, skills, and expertise. You are a hidden literary treasure, my friend.

Thanks always to Regina (Robinette) Fleming-Dobbins, Marquitta Mason White, Quandra' Swayze, Carolyn Denise Rooks, Yvette Williams, Tiffany Davis, LaDetria Titus, and Tasha Parker. Readers and supporters like you make what I do worthwhile and help me to be successful!

Shelia E. Bell

one

"I can take your man if I want to." Mahogany Lox

Rianna paced across the creaking hardwoods of Apartment 3D. Hezekiah was supposed to have been there hours ago. He'd pulled this same disappearing act first three weeks ago, then last week, then a few days ago, and again tonight.

She shook her head as she peeped out the window at some kids in the apartment complex playing tag in the pot-holed lined street. Something was stinking; she could smell it! She'd been calling and texting him and he hadn't responded since earlier that day.

Her mind was plotting, thinking about where he was, what he was doing, and who he was doing it with. She sure as hell hoped he wasn't sneaking over to his ex-wife's house.

She was nobody's fool. Rianna could tell Hezekiah still had feelings for Fancy. When Fancy's boyfriend got killed, Hezekiah ran straight to Fancy to comfort her, or that's how he explained it. Why wouldn't he check on her? He and Fancy shared history, a lengthy history. That history was the main freaking reason Rianna was against him moving into the same community where Fancy lived. She thought of a conversation they'd had about this a few weeks ago.

"I told you, New Holy Rock Ministries will cover the lease, nothing out of my pocket. You can imagine how nice the place is. I mean, we're talking Lion's Gate. Plus, it'll give me time to decide if I want to buy another house or not."

1

"Yes, but it's in the same neighborhood where your ex-wife lives, baby," Rianna said calmly, trying to sound concerned without saying what she really felt. "And what about, Pastor Stiles, your brother? Why can't he move into Lion's Gate instead? I mean, he is the assistant pastor."

"I told you, Stiles just signed his new lease on his spot, and he's content living where he is, for now," Hezekiah said impatiently. "And as for my ex? Baby girl, you have nothing to be jealous of. She's my ex-wife for a reason."

"I still don't like it." She huffed.

"Okay, what if I hold off a couple months? I'll stay where I am and pray on it some more."

"Oh, baby, I love you! And you can always live here. I know it's not much, but it's quiet over here, nobody all up in your business."

"We'll see. I might do that."

Rianna shook off the thoughts and went to her bathroom. Standing in front of the mirror and resting both palms on top of the granite vanity, she bit down on her bottom lip, frowned, and shook her head.

"Hezekiah McCoy!" she seethed like a mad woman. "Where the heck are you? Talkin' 'bout I don't have nothin' to be jealous over. That's a bunch of bull—and you know it," screaming at herself in the mirror.

She turned and rushed out of the bathroom, went back in the living room, retrieved her cell phone, and plopped down on her deep cushioned sofa. Again, she texted him, and followed up with a phone call to his cell phone. Like the times before, Hezekiah did not answer.

O

"May I use your bathroom?"

2

Fancy weakly pointed over her left shoulder. "It's up the hallway, on the right.

Hezekiah checked his phone when he entered Fancy's bathroom. Rianna wouldn't stop blowing him up. He shot her a quick text.

"@hospital visiting a sick member. Call you as soon as I can.

Hopefully his text would quieten Rianna's behind down. He didn't need a jealous, out of control, psycho woman chasing after him. He had to get her in check, let her know he was not going to be confined. His ministry wouldn't allow it and neither would his flesh.

After sending the text, he switched his phone to SILENT and refocused his attention on his ex.

He walked back into the quiet, dimly lighted living room.

Stepping up, closing any gap between them, he tenderly embraced Fancy and whispered, "You're a wreck. I hate to see you like this."

Fancy succumbed to his touch, resting against his chest, allowing his massive hands to travel the familiar course of her spine.

"I'll be fine," she finally managed to say, weakly, while pulling away from him.

"Maybe I should stay the night," he offered.

She looked at him strangely, her brows rose with a dreamlike gaze. *Don't do anything stupid, Fancy. You're just in your feelings about Micah.*

In her feelings or not, her body told her what her lips refused to openly admit.

"No, you should leave." She pushed him away, but not with much conviction. Then a light bulb came on. "I wouldn't want Rianna to come looking for you," Fancy jabbed.

"I'm my own man. You should know that better than anyone," Hezekiah shot back.

3

"How could you do this? I can't believe you." Fancy eyed him in disbelief before turning away and looking out the double glass patio door at the lake. "Wait a minute, what am I thinking? Yes, I *can* believe you would manipulate her to get what you want." She turned back to him spitting the word out.

Hezekiah straightened up, stiffened a bit, but remained silent. He allowed her to continue her banter. He knew Fancy. If she had no one to argue back with her, she would settle down in no time.

"I saw you, you know."

"You saw me? What on earth are you talking about, woman?"

"I saw you out in the church vestibule the day of Khalil's wedding. You were all up in Rianna's ear. For God's sake, Hezekiah, have you no shame? She's the freaking choir director. She's certainly not...well, who am I to say anything?"

Hezekiah looked at Fancy. His smile wasn't really a smile. It was something between a smile and a sneer.

"I don't know what you're talking about." He held her eyes for a moment. "Was I at our son's wedding? Of course I was there. I wouldn't miss that day for anything, even though I wasn't invited. Granted, that boy has done some scandalous things against me, but he's still my son. I love him no matter what."

"You may love him, but I know you all too well, Hezekiah. You still blame him for the money you say came up missing. Sabotaging his wedding day was one way of getting back at him. But, you forgot something."

Hezekiah remained silent, but he was quite curious to hear what else Fancy was about to tell him.

"You forgot your son is a chip off the old block. He's definitely his father's son because despite your cunning to ruin his day, he still married the girl of his dreams."

This time Hezekiah broke out into laughter. "Girl of his dreams? Come on now! You must have a concussion because you're talking crazy!"

Even Fancy laughed. Not as loud, but still he did what he had always been able to do—bring a smile to her face and a bit of laughter in her heart.

two

"Jealousy in romance is like salt in food. A little can enhance the savor, but too much can spoil the pleasure and, under certain circumstances, can be life-threatening." Maya Angelou

"Where were you? I texted you all night and you didn't answer. I was worried about you," Rianna said, whining.

"I told you, I was with a sick church member, When I didn't answer after you kept hitting me up, that should have told you something." Hezekiah was trying to keep calm, but the last thing he needed or wanted was someone to keep a check on him like he was a kid or something.

Remaining quiet, Rianna rolled her eyes and bit down on her bottom lip while holding the phone to her ear like it was stuck.

"You still could have text me back," she said, in almost a whisper.

"Look, I'm not going to do this, Rianna. I told you from the start, I don't do well with clinginess and jealousy. I'm a pastor. I am at the beck and call of God and his people. I can be gone for hours at a time ministering to His people. There'll be times when I can't answer your call or text. Now if you can't handle that, then this is the time for you to walk away."

Rianna didn't like it, but she listened as she stood looking out the window of Apartment 3D. She maintained her inner wave of mixed emotions because she didn't want to run Hezekiah off. Though she'd heard every word he said, she didn't quite believe it one hundred percent. Her thing was

6

New Holy Rock Ministries wasn't opening its church doors until the following week, and he didn't have a slew of members. So who was he babysitting tonight?

She told herself to get a grip. She had to play this hand right if she wanted to walk down the aisle and become the First Lady of New Holy Rock.

"I'm not jealous, Hezekiah," she lied. "I was just concerned about you, baby. I wanted to make sure you were ok. You know how these Memphis streets are," she cooed.

"Yeah, I hear you. Well, look I'm about to take a shower and get dressed. I have to meet my brother at the church at eleven."

"Okay, are you coming over later?" she asked, hoping this time she didn't sound like she was pleading.

"Yes, I'll hit you up when I'm on my way. You going to work today?"

"Nope, I don't have to go until tomorrow afternoon."

"Cool. Then I'll be over soon as I'm done. Oh, and while I'm out, I need you to make sure I have something to help me relax when I get over there."

"You know I got you," Rianna said and sent him a smacking kissy sound over the phone. "I'll see you soon."

Hezekiah responded by ending the call. Rianna was a cool girl and all, but she had a long long way to go if she ever planned on reaching Fancy's level. No woman had ever done to him what Fancy did and still managed to do. She had him hooked for life, yet she had no idea. Hezekiah wanted to keep it that way. Some women tend to get crazy when you let them know how you feel about them.

As for Rianna, just like the other women who had ventured in and out of his life, she was temporary. A temporary fix until he could get into a

7

permanent situation with who knows, maybe Fancy again.

three

"You can only be jealous of someone who has something you think you ought to have yourself." Margaret Atwood

Rianna read a number of online articles and social media posts about the murder-suicide involving Fancy McCoy. She read a couple of captions out loud to her friend and co-worker, Tiny, who was visiting.

"But they haven't really said what the relationship was between her and the doctor and why she was at his house," Tiny said.

"I know, right. The dead woman was his ex-wife."

"Right, and the man who killed her and the doctor was her boyfriend. They say he had beat her up really bad and put her in the hospital recently. At least that's what one of the clickbait articles said."

"So what do you think of the former First Lady of Holy Rock? She's not so perfect after all, huh?"

"Not by a long shot. Then again who is?"

The friends laughed.

"I'm going to make it my mission to find out what's really up with Miss First Lady. I have this feeling Hezekiah has seen her, talked to her or something since this stuff went down."

"Why do you say that?" Tiny asked.

"I just do, that's all. And he moved in the same gated community where she lives so he could easily have gone over to her house when he heard about the shooting."

9

"What? Did you say he moved in her neighborhood?"

"Yep."

"Ummmm. Well, I don't guess that's anything wrong with that. He told you, so it's not like he's hiding anything, right?"

Rianna didn't respond. She got up from the sofa and disappeared into the kitchen.

Tiny took the last swallow of her glass of alcohol, got up and followed Rianna.

In the kitchen, Rianna was preparing her own glass of alcohol.

"You want more?" She asked.

Tiny walked up and extended her glass toward Rianna.

Rianna poured until Tiny showed her palm. "Thanks."

"So, like I said, he told you he moved over there so he wasn't hiding anything." Tiny watched her closer.

"Who says he told me?" Rianna looked away.

Tilting her head, Tiny's small eyes narrowed. "So if he didn't tell you, how do you know where he lives?"

Rianna smirked, and brought the liquor to her lips and did not bring it away until her glass was empty.

She shook her head like a dog shaking off water. "If I tell you, I might have to kill you." She laughed hysterically.

Tiny joined in the laughter while shaking her head. "You know you're crazy."

"Yep, tell me something I haven't heard before."

four

"Be happy in front of your haters;
it kills them." Unknown

"In celebration of this first Sunday back in the Lord's house, we're asking for a special love offering to God to show our gratitude to Him for keeping us safe during this past year and thus far. You know some folks didn't make it," Khalil preached, parading back and forth across the front of the sanctuary.

The congregation was on their feet praising God and taking money down to the front of the church. Some of them came and laid money directly on the steps of the altar while others placed their money into wicker baskets lined across the front of the sanctuary.

"Sista Rianna, will you please lead the choir in a song of praise. Let's thank the Lord for the marvelous things he has done!"

Rianna Jamison led the choir in praise and then turned and directed the congregation to stand to their feet and join in.

Fancy watched, slightly shaking her head, not from praising God but from feeling disgust toward Rianna. She knew beyond a shadow of a doubt Rianna was sleeping with Hezekiah. She told herself she had no reason to be jealous. She and Hezekiah were divorced and he'd done enough vile things to keep her disliking him for a lifetime.

Yet, just last night she had let him into her house again. He showed up, ringing her doorbell, once again, with the excuse he was just checking in to make sure she was good.

11

Nothing happened, but it wasn't because her body wasn't on fire for him. She just restrained herself by not allowing him to come past the foyer.

Rianna swished back and forth across the pulpit, like she was directing a symphony orchestra.

She was good at what she did and no one could tell her anything different.

She could feel Fancy's eyes pinned on her. She loved and enjoyed every moment of it.

Let her sit out there with her uppity new daughter-in-law and envy me because I have what she knows she wants. But Hezekiah will never be hers again. Not as long as I'm around, and I don't plan on going anywhere.

Rianna raised her hands even higher in the air, prancing across the pulpit, and directing the choir to sing with all their mighty voices—and they did.

After the end of church services, Rianna went to the choir room, made sure all the robes were returned to their hangers, and that all hymnals were in their proper section before she left Holy Rock.

Walking along the hallway, she spoke to several other staff and some lingering church members as she proceeded toward the exit.

"Rianna, Sista Rianna," someone called.

Rianna turned in the direction of the voice coming from behind her. It was Fancy.

I knew it. Let's see what she has to say. Rianna gloated to herself.

"How can I help you, First Lady?" Rianna said. Although she no longer held the position of First Lady, most people at Holy Rock continued to address Fancy as such.

"Do you have a minute? There's something I'd like to talk to you about," Fancy said.

"Uh, sure."

"Let's step into my office," Fancy said, and headed toward her office.

Stepping into Fancy's office, Rianna continued to smirk as she trailed Fancy.

"Have a seat," Fancy offered, pointing to one of two fuchsia fabric covered chairs.

"Thanks, but I'm good."

"Suit yourself. So I'll get straight to the point."

"And the point is?" said Rianna, suddenly feeling herself, and crossing her arms.

"Are you sleeping with my ex-husband?" Fancy asked directly, looking into Rianna's eyes, and studying her expression.

This was exactly what Rianna loved—drama.

"No disrespect, *Mizzus McCoy,*" Rianna said, knowing this would no doubt irritate Fancy. "but who I'm sleeping with is really none of your business. I'm the choir director. I don't see where or how my personal life should be of any concern to you or anyone at Holy Rock for that matter."

"You think you're something else, but you don't know who you're messing with. So, I'm asking you again...are you sleeping with Hezekiah?"

"And I'm telling you again, it's none of your business. Now, if that's all you wanted to know, then I'm outta here." Rianna huffed, turned around, and headed for the door.

Fancy moved swiftly, jumping in front of the door. "I know you and Hezekiah had something to do with sabotaging my son's wedding, but if you think Hezekiah really wants you, you are more stupid than I give you credit for," Fancy retorted.

"You don't scare me." Rianna brazed up in her chest. "You're just jealous because he doesn't want your broke down behind anymore."

"Get out of here!" Fancy yanked open her office door. "When Khalil hears about this, you're gone. Wait, you know what?" Fancy paused and looked

13

her straight in the eye. "I forgot, I don't have to wait on Khalil to tell you what I have the authority to do myself! You're fired!"

Rianna looked at Fancy like she wanted to break her into a thousand pieces. Looking directly at her, she said, "No, you sure don't have to wait on the Pastor. And you can't fire me because I quit!"

Rianna zoomed past the front office so fast, leaving nothing but the sound of high heels click-clacking on polished concrete floors as she exited through the doors leading to the parking lot.

"Lord, what's going on now?" Sista Mavis jumped up from behind her desk and rushed to the door just in time to see Rianna getting into her car. Talking to herself and shaking her head, Sista Mavis chuckled. "Humph, guess you musta bit off more than you can chew."

five

"My silence is not weakness, but the beginning of my revenge." Unknown

Hezekiah and Stiles ended the first official Sunday service of New Holy Rock Ministries on a high note. Stiles was equally, if not more, surprised than Hezekiah to see all the people who attended. Five people and one couple came forward and joined the church.

Standing at the foot of the pulpit talking about the success of Sunday service, the brothers were interrupted.

"Hum, uh, excuse me." Rianna walked into the sanctuary, lingering in the doorway before walking up to Hezekiah and Stiles.

"Hey, how are you?" Hezekiah asked, looking stunned to see Rianna.

"I'm sorry to interrupt, but I need to talk to you," she said, looking briefly at Stiles before switching focus to Hezekiah.

"Hello, Sista Rianna," Stiles said, leaning in and giving her a light hug. "It's good to see you."

"Same to you, Pastor Graham."

"Look, bruh, you two talk. I'm going to my office and pick up something I left and then I'm headed out of here. You straight?"

"Yes, I'm good. We'll talk later."

"Sista Rianna, take care and God bless." Stiles proceeded to walk toward the exit of the sanctuary while Rianna positioned herself next to Hezekiah.

"What's up?" Hezekiah asked as soon as Stiles disappeared. "Service over at Holy Rock?"

15

"Yes. I just thought you'd want to know that your ex-wife just fired me!" Rianna huffed, and tears quickly appeared in the corners of her deep brown eyes.

Hezekiah grabbed hold of her elbow and led her out of the sanctuary, up the hallway, and to his office.

Closing his office door, Rianna followed him. Hezekiah sat in his brown high back leather office chair and Rianna took the seat in front of his desk.

"Now what's going on? What do you mean Fancy fired you? Why would she do something like that?"

"Guess." She stared at him with a smirk look on her face.

Hezekiah looked puzzled. "Uh, I don't know," he said extending both hands out.

"She accused me of sleeping with you. Came right out and asked me if I was."

Hezekiah raised both hands, clasped them, and rested his head into them as he leaned back.

"She asked you that?" he said, startled.

"She sure did, and when I told her I didn't think my personal business should be any concern to her, she fired me! That wanch has some nerve."

His outside appearance didn't reflect what he was feeling on the inside. He smiled inside, knowing Fancy was jealous and still had feelings for him. After their encounter a couple of nights before when he paid her a visit, he knew then that she still had mad love for him, but today cemented it. Hearing Rianna tell him the extent Fancy went to question her and then fire her, made today even better than it already was.

"And what did that son of mine have to say about it?"

"Nothing, yet. I don't guess he knows. It just happened and I left and came straight here." She wiped back her forced tears with the back of her hand. "I don't know what her problem is. She was accusing me of being in cahoots with you to sabotage Pastor Khalil's wedding."

Hezekiah chuckled.

"What are you laughing at? I just lost my position and you're laughing?"

"Come *ooon*," Hezekiah joked, "it's not that bad. You were just the choir director. It's not like that's your main bread and butter."

"Well, I don't agree. I need that job. It helps pay the bills, and it's what I enjoy doing the most. You think I like working in retail? No, I do not."

"If it'll make you feel any better, you can be the choir director here. I need to have someone who can help build up the choir, make it the best in the city. Or better yet, you want to be the minister of music?"

"Hezekiah? The minister of music?" She squealed and jumped up and down in place. "Are you serious?"

"You darn right I'm serious."

"Oh, my God. Thank you, baby! Thank you *sooo* much!"

Hezekiah and Rianna stood up. Hezekiah walked over to where she was and pulled Rianna into his arms, and started kissing her right in the middle of his office.

"Whaddaya say we christen New Holy Rock Ministries."

17

six

"One lie is enough to question all truths."
Quotesgram

Rianna lounged around in Apartment 3D, still reveling over the fact she was the minister of music for New Holy Rock Ministries, her man's church! Everything was falling into place. The argument with Fancy that led to her being fired from Holy Rock was, for her, one of those *blessings in disguise* and she couldn't be happier.

Fancy McCoy had dug a ditch for herself and now Rianna was one step closer to becoming First Lady of New Holy Rock Ministries. She only had to keep playing her cards right. No mess-ups, no hiccups, no wrong turns. She had to be on point.

The knock on the door pulled her from her thoughts.

"Big Daddy," she said, grinning large and looking down at the little man standing before her on the other side of the door.

The stocky, silver-haired dwarf strolled into her apartment confidently, like he towered six feet instead of being less than four feet tall. Entering the apartment, he helped himself to the ottoman, which was the perfect height and size for him to sit on.

"What you got for me today?" she asked, sitting down on the sofa across from Big Daddy.

"This." He removed his black backpack, pulled out a sealed nine by ten brown envelope, and passed it over to Rianna.

Rianna carefully opened the envelope. She displayed a huge smile on her face when she saw the contents inside.

18

Scanning through the pages, she paused and looked over at the man who had pulled out a cigarette, lit it, and took several draws.

"You know I hate it when you smoke in my house," she reminded him.

"With what I just delivered, you shouldn't care what I do up in here. I just helped you out a whole lot."

"I hope so."

"Hope? Sweetheart, you don't have to hope. Did you see what I gave you?" The man laughed, took a draw from his cigarette and then stood. Walking over into the kitchen area, he unsuccessfully tried to turn on the faucet. Rianna walked over and assisted him.

"Let me do that," she said and ran the cigarette underneath the stream of water before tossing it into the nearby trash bin.

One thing that made things work out between her and Big Daddy the dwarf, whose given name was Abel, was the fact he was married.

Abel's wife lived in a huge house on Puget Sound. Abel frequented Memphis and the South because he was born in North Memphis and one of his two tire stores was located in Collierville.

Born a dwarf, and being the only white boy in a tough, all-Black neighborhood, he grew up fast. He earned his respect in the streets, took his share of beatings, bullying and taunting, but persevered until he excelled in the streets and became one of the top plugs in the city.

Those days he'd mostly put behind. He invested the dirty money he made in the streets into legal businesses, and here he was today, legally rich and powerful—*mostly*.

Abel was an eccentric little man who didn't want someone who was all caught up in him. He had too many other irons in the fire and his

19

freakish ways wouldn't allow him to be linked to just one woman. He had the money to get any honey he wanted. For now, he wanted Rianna. Helping her with her investigation into her little preacher boyfriend was no big deal for him. The happier he made her, the happier she made him. He rather enjoyed helping her play I spy. It gave him another form of weird entertainment.

He liked his women like Rianna, slender, caramel with a wild streak. His wife, however, was just the opposite. She was an Asian *little person* like Abel, content to live the elaborate yet low-key lifestyle afforded her by her husband. Washington State was where she lived most of her life. It was home. She still had family there. What her husband did when he was away from home was no concern of hers.

Rianna had been Abel's quote unquote 'escort' going on two years. His connection with people from various backgrounds, and his deep money pockets, of course, is what drew Rianna to him. And she couldn't help but be intrigued a little bit about his height or lack thereof. She'd heard some wild and crazy stories about dwarf men and what good lovers they were supposed to be. Abel proved those stories to be on point, leaving her more than satisfied!

As long as it suited her financially, Rianna was not above engaging in illegal transactions. Not only that, Rianna was all about revenge. She was one of those people who carried a grudge—for a very long time.

"I'm going to wait before I open this, but believe me, I'm going to go through every piece of paper in that envelope with a fine toothed comb. Okay, so where's my other stuff?"

"Hey, don't get too feisty, there. You owe me. Don't get things twisted. You're not in charge here, baby."

Rianna slightly twisted her lips. She put the papers back inside the envelope, leaned over, and laid it on the table. Standing up, she walked up to him.

Just as she stood in front of him, he grabbed her arm and forcefully yanked her down to his level. His hands immediately began roaming all over her body while looking at her with a dirty old man look. A wicked smile spread across his face as his hands went to her most private place and began doing things to her she didn't like but had come to accept.

Rianna hated the feel of his fat, little grimy hands all over her body and touching her there, but she had to do what she had to do in order to get what she wanted. Like Malcom X said, "by any means necessary."

The man whose name was Abel, got down off the ottoman, and next, without saying a word, she took his little dwarf hand and led him all the way into her bedroom. She wanted to get this over quick, fast and in a hurry. She wasn't expecting Hezekiah until later that evening, when the sun went down, which gave her plenty of time to handle her business.

Night time visits were Hezekiah's signature MO. Sometimes he would pay her visit during daylight hours, but that was rare, very rare.

Inside her bedroom, the dwarf sat on a step stool at the side of Rianna's bed, kicking off his shoes, unzipping his dress slacks, and then he unbuttoned his shirt. The sly grin never once leaving his silver bearded face as he removed every stitch of clothing.

21

He then tugged at Rianna's clothing. "Take 'em off. What are you waiting for?"

"Hol' up, where's my other package? No goodies until you deliver *all* the goodies," she said adamantly, taking a step back from him.

Grunting, he stood, almost tripping over his pants and boxers that were still gathered around his ankles.

Kicking them off, he got up and darted into the living room, retrieved his backpack, and returned to the bedroom with a small plastic sandwich bag filled with white powder.

He almost drooled on himself when he saw Rianna laid back on the bed fully naked and exposed. Abel could barely hold back his sexual excitement.

He walked over to the bed and gave Rianna the baggie.

Rianna reached for the plastic bag, opened it, and tested a small portion by scooping some of the powder onto her long manicured fingernail. Tasting it, she looked at him as if giving him permission to do what it was he wanted.

He smiled and then proceeded climbing on the step stool.

Seeing him having difficulty getting up into her king-sized bed, she stifled her laughter, not wanting to embarrass him. She reached out, and picked up the little man off the step stool and helped him onto her bed.

While he began using her body to pleasure himself, she laid back and thought of how pleased Hezekiah was going to be when he came through later that evening.

seven

"Each betrayal begins with trust." Martin Luther

Abel left Apartment 3D fully satisfied—for now. Rianna showered, made herself a PB&J sandwich, ate it, and then took a seat in Hezekiah's favorite chair.

She opened the brown envelope Abel had left for her. The plastic bag full of cocaine was on the table in arm's reach.

Taking a fingernail full of the powder, snorting it, she got up and took the rest of it in her room, placing it inside the drawer.

"Let's see what we have here," she said aloud when she returned to the living room. A hand flew over her mouth when she started reading the contents of the envelope.

"Dang, Big Daddy, you weren't lying; you came through big time! She continued reading the report.

"Hezekiah has a bastard kid! Oh, my God. I wonder if Little Miss Perfect Fancy and her punk sons know about this." She looked at the picture of the little boy standing next to a woman, man, and another kid. The picture had an arrow pointing to the woman with the word "Mommy" written on it in red ink. Another arrow pointed to one of the little boys with the name, "Bastard" written next to it.

She sulked momentarily. She wanted to be the one to give Hezekiah a kid. Seeing this little boy who looked about five or six years old, gave her a pause. Was he active in the boy's life? Was he still sleeping with the kid's mother? These were questions she would have to get Big Daddy to find out.

23

In the meantime, Rianna continued reading. There was so much information, it boggled her mind. Not only did Hezekiah have a kid outside of his marriage, she read all about George being on Hezekiah's payroll and was basically Hezekiah's bodyguard and goon. But she was even more shocked to read that Khalil had already gotten himself a chick on the side, and it was none other than Detria Graham, one of the former first ladies of Holy Rock.

"Pastor K, you just got married and you have a woman on the side already? I guess that stuck up, saditty wife of yours, must not be cutting it."

As for Detria, Rianna didn't personally know the woman, other than she used to be married to Stiles Graham, who was one of the pastors of Holy Rock a few years back, but was now associate pastor at New Holy Rock Ministries.

Rianna read in the report where Detria had had a kid with Pastor Stiles, but the little girl died in a car accident when Detria got in an altercation with her then lover's girlfriend.

"This chick is a real piece of work," Rianna said, flipping the paper to continue reading. "And she has a kid by the dude she was cheating on Stiles with. Detria, you sound like a first class bitch. Umm, and she's sitting on a pile of money too," Rianna learned. "Oh, I see," she said, continuing her conversation with self, "so she got a lawsuit settlement in the seven figures. Wow! No wonder Pastor Khalil is sleeping with the enemy. *Shhoood...*I don't blame ya. I ain't mad at ya, Pastor K."

Rianna laughed out loud, slapping her thighs as she had a field day reading all the top secret stuff Abel had collected.

Big Daddy had included addresses, names, even the type of cars, and all sorts of information on the Grahams and McCoys.

The laughter ended and she became especially disturbed to learn that Hezekiah hadn't told her the truth about a lot of things.

A hand flew to her mouth when she read the paperwork showing Hezekiah had leased a five bedroom house in the exclusive Lion's Gate, the private gated community where Fancy lived. This pissed her off to no end because he told Rianna he wouldn't move there after she told him how uncomfortable it made her feel. Not only had he moved there, the house was huge. As far as she knew, until now, he was supposed to be still living in the small rental near New Holy Rock Ministries.

"So this is how you play, Hezekiah? Okay, so be it. But I'm not the one, baby. I'm not weak like Fancy McCoy. Nah, I'm always going to be a step ahead of you."

She had the address, an image of the house, and even an access code to enter the gated community. Rianna didn't know how Abel was able to collect all the information he had, but she was not about to question him about his sources. All she needed him to do was keep feeding her information. In return, she would keep fulfilling his sexual fantasies. *A fair exchange*, she thought.

She reached next to her and picked up her phone from off the arm of the chair. "Tiny," Rianna said into the phone," girl, you won't believe all the tea I just found out."

"What is it! Tell me," urged Tiny. "What's going on?"

"It's too much; I can't tell you everything about it now."

25

"Dang, heffa, then you shouldn't have called me. You know I want the scoop! My kid says I'm nosy, and he ain't lyin'."

"I know, but Hezekiah will be here in a minute and I need to finish getting ready, but I'll call you tomorrow 'cause girl, do I have some tea to spill with you."

eight

"Something I learned about people. If they do it once they'll do it again." Quotesideas.com

Rianna sat on the sofa in Apartment 3D, crossing and uncrossing her legs repeatedly. Where in the heck was Hezekiah? She tried calling him again, but there was no answer. She texted again, no answer.

A knock on her door startled her. She hurried to the door, and peeped through the peep hole. Her countenance went from a frown to a smile when she saw Hezekiah on the other side.

Quickly, she unlocked and opened the door. She swooped him, wrapping her arms around him as soon as he crossed the threshold of Apartment 3D.

"Where have you been? I was worried. You said you were on your way but that was over two hours ago!"

Hezekiah gave her a *you know better than to ask me where I've been* look.

Rianna immediately backed off.

He kissed her and then walked all the way into the apartment.

Rianna closed the door behind him. Dressed in a fire red thong and skimpy red bra, she slithered over to where he stood, touching him in all the places she knew would arouse him.

Hezekiah stepped out of her grasp and turned to look at her or right past her. "Not now. Look, I'm sorry, but I can't stay. There's been an emergency with one of the members."

27

"But you just got here," she said, sadly disappointed.

"Did you get it?" he asked, looking around like he was fiending for something and not bothering to acknowledge what she'd just said.

"Yea." She slowly turned around and went and retrieved the plastic bag. She bumped into his chest when she was returning with the bag, not knowing Hezekiah had walked up behind her.

He removed the bag from her hand. "Thanks, sweetness!" He kissed her deeply, and then opened the packet and took several deep snorts of the powder.

After a couple of minutes, he said, "You did good, baby. This is fire."

"I'm glad it gets your stamp of approval."

He grabbed Rianna, kissed her again, while squeezing her butt.

"Dang, baby, I wish I could stay. I really, really do but I can't, not tonight. You understand, don't you?"

"Why do you have to go?" she whined. "Can't you go and do whatever it is you need to do and then come back?" she pleaded.

"I don't think so. Whenever I'm done, I'm going to want to crash afterwards. I have a long week."

"You can always crash here. You know that. And you said this is your sanctuary, your place of peace when you need to get away from the hustle and bustle of life." She cooed, rubbing her body up against him.

Hezekiah found himself becoming sexually aroused. "See what you do to me?" His eyes shifted briefly below. "This is exactly why I can't stay and why I can't come back. I wouldn't be able to keep my hands off you. I wouldn't get a moment's rest."

Rianna made it difficult for Hezekiah to resist, but he had to get out of there. He didn't want to waste his high or his libido on Rianna. Not tonight. He had other things on his mind and someone else he planned to help him along the way. That person was not Rianna.

nine

"The way I see it, if you want the rainbow you gotta put up with the rain." Parade.com

"Victoria, I don't know why I did it," Fancy said, whispering into her phone like someone else was in the house with her eavesdropping.

"You did it because you've suffered a tremendous loss. You're lonely, you're grieving, and you needed someone other than this fair-weather friend by your side."

"Stop it, Victoria. You are not a fair-weather friend; you're my *best* friend. If you want to call anybody fair-weather, it should be me. I feel like I bailed on you when you and Pepper needed me the most."

"That's not true and you know it, but anyway, we aren't going back down that road tonight. You have to decide what you're doing, Fancy. Hezekiah took advantage of you. You may not agree, but that's how I see it. And you know me; I'm going to be honest with you, not just tell you what you want to hear. You and Hezekiah, I just don't know if that's a good thing."

"I know you don't, and to keep it one hundred with you, I don't know how I feel about it either. Then again, like you said, I'm lonely and I miss Micah so much. God, I still can't believe he's gone, Victoria. And you didn't even get the chance to know him, I mean really know him. He was such a beautiful man with a sweet spirt and an abiding love for God."

"God rest his soul. I wish I could have gotten to know him too, but God had other plans for him

30

and for you. I just don't know if those plans for you included you and Hezekiah hooking up."

ten

"Nothing in the world can trouble you like your own thoughts." Littlenivi.com

Fancy played the conversation with Victoria over and over in her mind. What was she doing? Why did she even let Hezekiah get that close to her? Why did she let him into her house anyway? She knew she was weak for him. Always had been. In spite of all the things he'd done to hurt her, she still had love for the man.

She tossed a load of laundry in the dryer, then retreated to the kitchen and poured herself a glass of wine. While the clothes were drying, she sat on the sofa, turned on the television, and surfed channels until she stopped on one of her favorite reality shows.

Curling up on the sofa, she nodded a little and watched TV a little. The doorbell ringing startled her.

She couldn't imagine who it could be. The boys hadn't said anything about stopping by when she talked to them earlier in the day.

"Comiiing," she said when the doorbell rang a third time.

On the other side of the glass door stood her greatest temptation.

o

"How do I let you talk me into these things?" Tiny complained from the passenger's side of Rianna's white Kia Forte.

32

"Because you love me." Rianna laughed and made a right turn leading toward Lion's Gate.

"I love you, that may be true, but I don't love you enough to go to jail with you!" Tiny rebutted and laughed too.

"Girl, please, we are *not* going to jail. We're not breaking the law. All we're doing is seeing if he's at this house he swears he didn't move into, but Big Daddy says different."

"Girl, you so crazy. Don't call that man that.What's his real name anyway? I forgot."

Rianna looked over at Tiny, shook her head, and chuckled. "You lying. You know that man's name 'cause you're the one that introduced us."

"I did not. Not really. You saw him at my check out register and when he saw you, he flirted with you and bingo, now he's your sugar daddy, sugar dwarf, Big Daddy, whatever."

"Okay, his name's Abel."

"As in Cane and Abel? Oh, shoot." Tiny laughed again. "Sounds like trouble. I don't know how I could have forgotten a name like that."

Rianna continued driving. She drove two short blocks, made another right and then a quick left. The last turn she made led her to the entrance of Lion's Gate. The guard shack was empty. That was a relief. Had there been a guard on duty, it was unlikely she would have gotten in.

She pulled out her phone and read the access code she'd gotten from Abel.

Pressing the window button, the window came down and Rianna entered the access code into the panel.

Bingo, the gate slowly swung open.

"Girl, my heart is racing!" Rianna said as she slowly drove into the neighborhood. "Okay, let me see...I should be coming to his house now." Rianna

33

drove slowly down the deserted street, reading the addresses as she went and listening to her GPS.

"And what exactly are you going to do if you find out he *really has* moved into this house?"

"I don't know, probably nothing. At least not right now. I just want to see something. See if he's a liar or if he can be trusted. And I really wanna see if that raggedy ex-wife of his is trying to sink her dirty claws back into him. This is it," Rianna said, repeating the address aloud.

"Dang, this crib is fire!" Tiny said. "Looks like a mini-mansion."

"I don't see any lights on."

"Wait, look, I do," chimed Tiny. Pointing slightly to her right. "See, looks like there's a light on in what could be the kitchen."

"Dang, and I can't tell if he's in there or not. He may be parked in the garage."

"Yeah, that's a three car garage, girl. This house is banging."

"Yeah, it is. And I can't wait to be living in it as First Lady McCoy."

"I heard that," said Tiny. "Speak it into existence!"

"What now? I mean, we don't know if he's in there or not or if he even lives there. They may have a light on just to make it look like someone lives there to keep people from breaking in."

"Girl, I don't think it would be that easy to break in here. This community is guarded and most of the time there's an actual human person at the front entrance."

Rianna remained outside in front of the house.

"Okay, are we just going to sit here or what?" questioned Tiny.

"Girl, will you chill out. Stop being so shaky."

"I'm not being shaky, just don't want to get involved in no mess. I still have six more months to go on my probation. I can't be caught doing nothing that even looks like it's illegal."

"Okay, okay, I've seen enough anyway. I guess we'll go. But I do want to see one more thing."

"What's that?"

"I wanna see where that heffa's house is," Rianna said. "What's her address?" Rianna looked at her phone again, scrolling through her gallery where she'd taken a screenshot of the paper Abel gave her with the information on it.

"It should be right around this....there it is."

Rianna came to an abrupt stop when she saw Hezekiah's midnight black Bentley parked in Fancy McCoy's driveway.

eleven

"Revenge sounds so mean, that's why I prefer to call it "returning the favor." Unknown

Rianna hit and yanked the steering wheel twice then cursed. She took a deep breath and started talking so fast, her words were getting tangled up.

"Slow down girl," Tiny said wiping flying spit out of her face. "Was that Japanese or something?" Tiny leaned closer to the door, clutching the handle. She pushed her blond bangs from her small face to the side.

"I knew that stanky heffa wanted him back. I knew it!" Rianna yelled.

"Just get outta here before somebody calls the cops." Tiny's voice shook. "I don't want no trouble. Six months and I'll be free. Ain't nothin' gonna mess that up for me."

Rianna made a U turn and burned a little rubber. Tiny stared at her friend as if she just couldn't understand what was going on in her head.

"I don't get it. Why you so mad at her and not at him? He's supposed to be your man, right? Ain't he the one that lied to you?" Tiny shook her small head as they drove towards her apartment.

Rianna didn't answer, and Tiny really didn't care as long as she ended up at home and not in jail.

Arriving at her apartment, Tiny got out of the car. "I'll see you at work tomorrow. Gnite." Tiny shut the door and took off up the stairs, two by two, leading to her apartment.

36

Rianna drove in silence the short distance to her apartment. Once inside Apartment 3D, she stripped, leaving a trail of clothes on the floor and headed to the bedroom. Tonight was like a bad scene in a horror movie. She was exhausted and needed to rest. She crawled between the cotton sheets naked and drifted off.

o

The blinding morning sunlight steamed through the blinds, forcing her to open her eyes and get out of bed.

She dragged herself into the bathroom or her *sanctuary* as she called it. Scented candles, sage, incense, plush towels, lush floor rugs, and a pastel colored wall made the small space look like a mini spa, and she loved it.

Rianna rubbed the puffiness of her eyes. "Not gonna happen, not on my watch," she said, standing in front of the bathroom mirror. She rather enjoyed or had a thing about standing in her bathroom mirror and holding full, in-depth conversations with herself. It somehow relaxed her, made her think she wasn't alone. She had friends like Tiny, but that was about it. She didn't have a good relationship with her parents, never had, and her siblings were living in other states doing their own thing. Yep, she was the black sheep of the family and no one could tell her different. But it was good, all good. She didn't need them anyway.

She finished getting dressed for work. This week she was scheduled to work first shift. Although she didn't like the early morning shift, she resigned herself to doing what needed to be done for now. Until she became the First Lady, she told herself she had to endure a few hardships. Working

37

behind a counter was included in those *hardships*. It would all be over once she said *I do*.

"Did you talk to him?" Tiny asked when Rianna arrived to work.

"Yea, I did, but I didn't tell him I saw him at Fancy's house." She turned and headed toward the back of the store.

Tiny followed. "What? Why not?" she urged.

Rianna placed a thumb under the time clock machine, and then turned back around facing Tiny. "You already clocked in?"

"Yea, right before you got here. So why didn't you say anything to him?"

"Think about it, I *couldn't* say anything or else he would know I had been snooping."

"True, but did he come over there last night, after we got back?" Tiny asked, looking puzzled.

"Nope. I didn't talk to him until a little while ago, before I came in here. He swore he was at home all evening. Said he had a couple of beers, watched the game, and passed out early. Girl, please, I know better than that. But it's all good."

"What's next then?" Tiny asked like an eager puppy waiting for a treat.

"You don't know half of what I have going on in this head of mine."

O

Rianna spent most of her shift texting Hezekiah and going back and forth with Abel. Hezekiah replied a couple of times.

The last text Rianna received from Hezekiah said, "comin by to pick up a li'l something b4 Bible study. C u ltr.

"Dang, I forgot Bible study was tonight," Rianna said aloud to no one other than herself. She had plans to see Big Daddy after she got off work.

Abel didn't demand a whole lot of her time, but by the same token he was the kind of man who was used to getting what he wanted. He had done quite well for himself. Being a dwarf hadn't kept him from accomplishing some huge monetary dreams. Abel owned and operated a lucrative online business, owned several brick and mortar tire stores, and one coffee shop. It went without saying that the little man had a boatload of money, probably millions.

He liked himself some Rianna. She played her hand well and gave him all the time he wanted, which usually meant seeing Abel once a week for their sexual rendezvous. He expected her to be his arm candy at social events.

Rianna had no problem with her role in Abel's life, except the fact she was now after Hezekiah and becoming increasingly disinterested in Abel. Yeah, Abel's money was long, and he took care of many of her financial needs. He spoiled her with expensive gifts, and he didn't mind doing her little dirty deeds, as long as she abided by his rules and granted him the desire of his little heart. That would all come to an end when she became the First Lady. She couldn't dare be caught being anything less than the woman of God she was expected to be.

twelve

"Be the kind of woman that makes every other woman want to be you." Topaz

Rianna did everything she could to keep from dozing off in Bible study, but it was hard, almost impossible, but she managed to keep her eyes from fully closing.

Immediately after work, she met Hezekiah, gave him his white packet of powder, and sent him off so she could hook up with Abel before leaving for Bible study.

Yep, she was exhausted beyond measure.

"God is not to be mocked," Stiles Graham's commanding baritone voice floated throughout the sanctuary.

Hezekiah sat on the front row of New Holy Rock Ministries, nodding in agreement with his brother's teachings.

Rianna caught him a time or two, looking over his shoulder, their eyes meeting.

At the end of Bible study, Hezekiah stood up and did something quite surprising.

"I want to officially announce and introduce to you, as I will also do this coming Sunday, our Minister of Music. Will you come forward or stand, Sista Rianna Jamison."

Hezekiah smiled and extended his hand toward Rianna.

Rianna stood, blushing from ear to ear. This was why she loved this man. He could be so thoughtful, so caring.

"Thank you, thank you, Pastor McCoy," she said shyly, and quickly took her seat.

40

"We're looking forward to some great things from you, Sista Rianna. I know you're going to make New Holy Rock choir the best in the state!" Hezekiah exclaimed and chuckled.

The congregation clapped and others said *Amen* and *Praise God* to Hezekiah's proclamation.

Stiles sat in the pulpit, clapping and thinking, *What happened to her being the choir director at Holy Rock? My brother is on a mission again, I see.*

Standing among some of the women married to ministers and deacons, Rianna inserted herself into their religious, holier-than-thou conversations.

How boring and fake they are, but I guess a First Lady's gotta do what a First Lady's gotta do.

She feigned laughter and added her own flavorful conversation to the group until she looked up and saw *her.*

"No this heffa didn't," Rianna cursed under her breath.

Fancy and some other lady Rianna didn't know were walking to the front of the sanctuary towards Rianna and her group. She and Fancy both connected eyes.

Fancy gave a wicked smile, and kept walking.

Rianna wanted to break from the group and go smack the mess out of her. She restrained herself, and instead watched Fancy.

Fancy said something to the woman who was walking beside her and then stopped when she was in front of Hezekiah and Stiles who were talking to two of the deacons.

Rianna watched as Fancy hugged Stiles. Stiles kissed her on the cheek and then repeated the act with the woman who was with Fancy.

Next, Hezekiah kissed Fancy on the cheek. Fancy hugged him for what seemed like an extra long time while rolling her eyes at Rianna.

Rianna was not to be intimidated. She sat on the back pew and waited while Hezekiah, Stiles, Fancy and the other lady talked, and talked, and talked...until there was no one left inside the sanctuary but them and Rianna.

Finally, she heard Fancy say rather loudly, "Of course, we'll be back," and laughed.

"Yes, we sure will," said the lady.

"I'm glad you came. I'll talk to you later, Victoria," Rianna heard Stiles say to the woman, leaning over and kissing her again on the cheek.

Umm, her name's Victoria, huh? Got to find out about her too. Those two seem a little cozy. Rianna made a mental note.

At that moment, Fancy and Victoria approached. Fancy stopped at the pew where Rianna was seated. She sneaked a quick peek over her shoulder like she was trying to see if Hezekiah noticed her talking to Rianna.

He didn't seem to notice because he was already in another conversation with one of the ministers and Stiles.

"So this is where the trash landed?" Fancy mocked, looking at Rianna and then at Victoria. "Oh, but they say one man's trash is another man's treasure."

Victoria tugged on Fancy's elbow. "Come on. She's not worth making a scene. You're a woman of God. She's just a Jezebel."

"You don't stand a chance," Fancy said, wickedly and pranced off and out of the sanctuary, leaving Rianna ready to exact vengeance.

thirteen

"You can't compete with the woman a man can't leave alone." Quotesgram

"Whoohooo, my stimulus check is in my account—all forty-two hundred dollars! Praise the Lord," Rianna exclaimed, jumping up and down in place.

"How did you get four thousand and something dollars when it's just you? You don't have any dependents."

"I told you to stop underestimating your girl," Rianna told Tiny over the phone. "I have my ways. Don't worry 'bout it."

"You're a piece of work. I got mine too, but it's already spent. I don't have a sugar poppa like you to keep me my head above water during this time. I'm just glad this country is basically back to normal."

"Yeah, me too. And I told you, I got you if you need to borrow a little something. I have to admit, Big Daddy has been taking real good care of me. I haven't missed a beat. And don't get me wrong, I'm not bragging. I'm just saying, God has been good."

"I'm glad for you, and yes I know I can come to you if I really needed to. But I'm glad we're considered essential workers. At least we haven't missed a paycheck. Even though we could probably get more if we collected unemployment. I know that's a shame to say, but it's the truth."

"Yeah, I know, but like you said, thank God this country is pretty much back to normal. Well, look, I gotta go. This is Big Daddy calling."

"Okay, buh-bye," said Tiny and the call ended.

43

"Hey, babe," she said to Abel.

"Do *I* have something for you. I'm telling you it's a bombshell."

"Oh, my God, what is it, Big Daddy? Stop teasing me. Is it a girl's best friend? You've given me so much already."

"No, I think you're going to like what I have better than diamonds," he teased.

"Oh, you've got me so nervous. Are you coming over or do you want me to come to your hotel?"

"You come to me tonight. I'll send a car for you. How long will it take you to get ready?"

"Give me an hour."

"Okay, I'll call when the driver is pulling up to your apartment."

"Okay."

"Oh, and baby?"

"Yes, Abel," Rianna cooed into the phone.

"I want to see just how bad you want what I have to give you. So come with your A game."

Rianna taunted, "I always do, baby. I always do."

○

"Are you smashing your ex-wife, Hezekiah? Tell me the truth," Rianna pressured.

"Look, do I make you happy?" He changed the subject immediately.

Rianna nodded. "You do."

"Do I make good love to you?" he asked, adding cream to the coffee.

"You do," she said, looking at him shyly and then bowing her head.

"Didn't I make you my Minister of Music?" he added with double sweetness.

Rianna nodded again.

44

Hezekiah walked up on her, removing her clothing as he continued manipulating her with his charming words.

"I like you. You know that. I like you a lot. I told you, I think I'm falling in love with you."

Rianna wanted to forget all about whether he was sleeping with Fancy or not, but she couldn't shake it. All she could see when she closed her eyes was Fancy telling her she would never have Hezekiah. She had to prove her wrong.

"If I make you happy, why do you have to mess with her? Why do you keep going back to her when all she's caused you is pain?" Rianna cried, sounding like a little girl instead of the full grown woman she was.

"You *do* make me happy, but I told you I don't like it when you act all jealous and out of whack. Okay, so I've seen my ex-wife a few times. So what? I think it's justified in light of what she's been going through lately. For God's sake, the woman's boyfriend and two other people were murdered in front of her. She's traumatized. As a pastor and as her ex-husband, the father of her children, I think it's only right that I be there to minister to her if and when she needs me. You, of all people, should understand that, Rianna. If you can't, then I don't know if you're cut out to be a First Lady. And as for her being at our Bible study, I told you I didn't invite her. She came with Stiles' lady friend, Victoria. But even if I *had* invited her, that's no reason for you to act anything less than respectful."

"I love you, Hezekiah. I want to be your wife. Don't you get that? I'm trying to be the woman you need, the woman you desire, but I can't compete with your past, especially your living past." Rianna pleaded with him to understand.

"And I've never asked you to, nor would I expect you to. This is not some competition. That's some crazy notion in your own head. Give me a reason, a good reason that I should even consider making you the First Lady of New Holy Rock Ministries. And don't say love, because love simply isn't enough."

"Okay, let's start here," Rianna said, peeling away the rest of her clothing.

fourteen

"Some women are once in a lifetime type of females; there is no upgrade after her." Unknown

"How much did you say?" Rianna asked the man. This wasn't exactly a stranger but he was no friend of hers either. She knew of him because he often hung around outside the pharmacy building where she worked.

"Five hundred."

"You *have* to be on crack or something 'cause you're crazy and high as hell if you think I'm going to pay you five hundred dollars just for striking a match."

"Suit yourself, but if you could do it yourself, or if you knew someone who would do it cheaper, then you wouldn't be talking to me."

Rianna stopped, looked at her cell phone, and then paused when the man kept talking.

"And I'm the one who would be taking the chance. I could go to the pen, and I don't wanna visit that place again, at least not right now. So what's it gonna be, lady?"

"Buster, I don't have time for this back and forth. I have to be inside this god awful place in five minutes. Are you going to do it or not? I'll give you two fifty and something to put up that raw nose of yours."

"Two fifty up front and two fifty when I do the job, and I still get a packet when I'm done," he insisted.

"Okay, okay, look, whatever. I can't argue with you anymore. I need this done. How soon can you do it?"

47

"How soon can you get me my money?"

"I'll get back with you." Rianna huffed and entered the store.

This day was definitely one to go down in the record books when Rianna looked up from her workstation and saw Fancy strolling through the pharmacy door.

Rianna was working in the Photo Department this week, which gave her a bird's eye view of just about every customer coming and going.

Fancy didn't come in her direction but went to the back of the store near the pharmacy.

Rianna strained to see her but lost sight of her when a customer approached the counter inquiring about his photos.

Rianna quickly waited on the customer and then looked past him. She was surprised to see Fancy standing behind the man.

"I need to talk to you," Fancy demanded.

"What do you want? Why are you here?"

Rianna was a step ahead of Fancy. She turned away from her, pretended like she was looking through a stack of photos but actually put her phone on RECORD. This was going to be a make it or break it point for Rianna. Ammunition to add to her growing arsenal.

"What are you doing here on my job?" Rianna asked, sounding suddenly like she was frightened.

"Girl, please, stop with all the theatrics. This is a business," Fancy shot back. "Anyway, I'm here because I want you to stay away from my family. I know what you're trying to do. You were in on trying to destroy my son's wedding. You're after my ex-husband, and you're all up in my business. I'm warning you. Stay away from us."

"I don't know what you're talking about. Please, if I've said or done anything wrong, please forgive me," Rianna's fake cry was getting attention.

Fancy looked around. A couple of customers had paused and were looking at her and Rianna.

"Can you take a break?" Fancy said.

Rianna called the cashier at the front and asked her to cover her station until she came from the bathroom.

"What do you want?" Rianna asked again, still recording their exchange. Only now they were in the back of the store in the Family Restroom.

Rianna locked the door from the inside.

"Now what is it you really want? I don't understand," Rianna pleaded with innocent eyes.

"I just told you. I want you to stay away from my family. Stay away from Hezekiah."

"So you *are* sleeping with him?" Rianna questioned. "Do your precious boys know you're going behind their backs and sleeping with the enemy? And what about Pastor Khalil? What about all that money he stole from his own father? What kind of sons did you raise anyway? One is a straight up thug and the other one is a flaming homosexual! What kind of sorry mother are you?"

Fancy reached out and slapped Rianna across the face so hard, it knocked Rianna against the tile covered wall, almost causing her to fall.

Rianna, as much as she wanted to, didn't retaliate. Instead, she screamed and cried.

"You hit me! You busted my lip! Why? Please stop, please I'm sorry for whatever you say I did. I won't see him again," she continued screaming.

Fancy looked, smirked and then spoke, "I told you, li'l girl, I'm not the one to play with. Find yourself another toy. And yeah, so what if I'm sleeping with him, huh? What are you gonna do about it?"

"You're pathetic," Rianna cried. "If Hezekiah knew this is how you were out here acting, he would have nothing else to do with you."

"Honey, I hope you don't think Hezekiah really cares about you. I know the man. I was married to him for years. I've been with him since we were teens. He's using you. Using you to get what he wants, and he wants *me*. Not you. You can carry out your little dastardly deeds for him all you want, but in the end, it'll get you nowhere. I can have him back in my bed anytime I want to. I've proven that. So remember that, sweetheart. And if you think that little role of yours as Minister of Music is going to last, you're even dumber than I thought. Now this is your first and last warning." Fancy spoke slow and deliberate. "Stay away from my family. Stay...away...from...Hezekiah."

Fancy stormed out of the bathroom, leaving Rianna standing in the middle of the cramped space with a satisfying grin on her face.

fifteen

"If you want me in your life, put me there. I shouldn't be fighting for a spot." Pinterest

Rianna gave Big Daddy what she called the *royal treatment*, which meant stopping at nothing to please him. He earned himself some extra goodies when he told her about Khalil's little bride being a convicted felon!

Rianna laughed and stomped around Apartment 3D like she'd just won the lottery.

"This is hilarious. First Lady Eliana Hodges has a rap sheet. I wonder if good ole Pastor Khalil knows. And you, Hezekiah, do you know your daughter-in-law is a felon?" she said aloud, like they were in the room with her and Abel.

Abel laid back in the king sized bed of his posh hotel suite and looked at Rianna. He liked to see her happy, to see her laughing, and especially to see her plotting. He may have been on the right side of the law now, pretty much, but he still had that yearning for a little badness in his life. Rianna brought that excitement. With her, he was always on the edge of his seat, always not knowing what to expect in the bedroom or when she was exacting revenge on someone who had dared to cross the path between what made her tick and what ticked her off.

"You think *that's* something? I'm telling you that's not even the icing on the cake," Abel said, patting the bed space next to him.

Rianna jumped back onto the bed, still butt naked, and landed right into his short but

51

muscular arms. Her body basically could cover his without hesitation.

Abel gathered her into his arms and began kissing and touching her. Rianna didn't hesitate to pleasure him again. Whatever Big Daddy wanted, Big Daddy got.

When they were done making love, Rianna eased up and sat upright in the bed, wiping back the hair from her face.

Abel climbed down out of the bed. Rianna kept a watchful eye on him to make sure he wouldn't fall. He had one of those hotel setups that finer hotels offered for little persons like Abel.

Like a little penguin, Abel waddled out of sight, disappearing into the master bath.

Rianna waited for him to return.

"Okay, what is it? Tell me, tell me." She bounced up and down on the bed like a happy kid in a candy shop. "What do you have for me?"

Abel stopped at the desk in the room and opened the top drawer. Pulling out a white business size envelope and another plastic bag filled with white powder, he walked over to Rianna's side of the bed, stood in front of her, and gave her the envelope and the bag.

"Thanks, Big Daddy. Get up here beside me." She patted the space in the bed next to her.

"Not now. I have a couple of calls to make. I'll be in the living room or outside on the balcony," he said and walked out of the massive three room space, leaving Rianna to go through the papers alone and to indulge in the nose candy.

"Here you go," Abel returned to the hotel room with a shot glass filled with Cîroc and passed it to her.

Rianna accepted the alcohol and leaned back against the headboard. "Thanks, babe."

"Yeah, okay, now off I go to make my calls."

"Hol' up," Rianna said, and leaned down and kissed Abel fully on the mouth. "When you get done with your calls, there's more where that came from," she teased.

O

A hand flew to her mouth when she read the explosive information. This was sure to give her the ace card. Hezekiah would easily marry her. With what she had, when she went to Hezekiah this next time, she was going to spill it all, tell Hezekiah everything, and she meant everything, except where she got her information and his drugs from.

If Hezekiah took her marriage idea as a proposition, so be it. She didn't care just as long as he accepted it. It didn't matter if he didn't love her or even if he was still in love with Fancy. What mattered was to gain his name. She would make him fall in love with her. Even if he didn't ever grow to love her, she was on her way to becoming the First Lady. With what she had, he would not only agree to marry her, he would be eternally grateful...if he had any sense.

sixteen

"Revenge...ohhhh what a sweet nectar it is."
Shelia Bell

Rianna was on the roll. It was time she showed whoever was in her path that she was a force to be reckoned with. First, she made a fake social media account and profile.

After she was done making the accounts, she pressed SEND with a feeling of total satisfaction and vindication. The direct message went to Khalil, to Holy Rock's church email where the nosey gossip and church secretary, Sista Mavis was sure to see it. Rianna also posted to the church's public social media pages, telling all about the new First Lady Eliana McCoy's criminal past. She even attached a copy of Eliana's rap sheet.

"Tiny, I had to do it. I had to send it. I'm dying over here," Rianna said. "Can you believe these hypocrites?" She laughed.

"No," Tiny's chubby hands flew to her mouth. "I know you didn't send that email, Rianna?"

"Yep, sure did.

"Girl, you for real crazy," said Tiny, amused by her friend's antics.

"Well, I'm not lying. Everything I posted is true. Eliana Hodges McCoy, Pastor Khalil's little ol' wife was sentenced to three years in the federal pen for assault, uh with a deadly weapon and attempted murder."

"Girl, you better stay out of her way then is all I'm going to say," Tiny joked.

Rianna laughed. "Anywho...now that I got that done, on to the next adventure. You riding or not?"

54

Tiny shook her head, but said, "I guess."

"Okay, I'll pick you up tonight, after I leave Bible study. Be ready."

o

The day was coming to a close. Rianna had been to choir rehearsal, attended Bible study, and now she and Tiny were parked outside Lion's Gate in a rental car.

"Are you sure about this?" Tiny asked, sweat dropping from her face like water. She kept looking behind her and from side to side. Tiny finally hit the door lock switch.

Rianna nodded. "Yep, as sure as I'll ever be. Only thing that'll make this fail is if he can't get inside the gate. He's probably gonna have to find an opening somewhere or get over that brick wall, and do what he was hired to do."

"Guess we'll know something soon enough," Tiny said, scooting down in the seat, making her already petite frame practically invisible to anyone who might look in their direction.

They were parked on the street in the back of Lion's Gate where Rianna could see a portion of Fancy's house. They sat inside the car in silence, holding their breath, waiting and watching for the show to begin.

Rianna was sure Fancy wasn't home. She and Tiny saw her car leave about an hour before. It was Bible study night at Holy Rock too, and Fancy hardly ever missed attending. Rianna assumed that's where Fancy was headed, which was the reason Rianna chose tonight for the action.

Sitting in the car for quite some time, nervous and excited at the same time, Rianna's eyes widened like giant hokey marbles when she saw a swirl of giant flames suddenly spiral through the air from the back of Fancy McCoy's house.

Tiny's hands flew over her opened mouth and her eyes grew big like saucers. "Oh, my God!" she screamed. "Look at it!"

After watching the flames light up the night sky like a fireworks display, Rianna inhaled deeply, slowly exhaled, while closing her eyes.

Next, her text notifier chimed. Rianna quickly opened her eyes, looked at her screen, and a smile appeared when she read the one word text, "DONE."

Rianna looked over at Tiny, laughed, and then quietly drove away. Sighing deeply, she pulled out into the main street.

"Yayyy, and another one bites the dust."

seventeen

"If it was manipulation; it was successful."
Unknown

"No, you're absolutely correct, you *don't* know me, but that's not the point. The point is...I know *you*. I know a whole lot about you *and* your husband," Rianna threatened, sitting across the table from the mystery woman.

Dressed like a runway model, Rianna smelled good, looked good, and talked like she was a Michelle Obama clone.

"You wouldn't want it to get out on your job, your kid's school, and those gossiping uppity women in your neighborhood and your church, for God's sake. Oh my, what would they say or do if they knew?" Rianna continued to torment the poor woman.

"If you don't tell me what it is you want and why you're threatening me, I'm calling the police. Right now. I mean it," the woman said, slightly pounding a fist on the table top inside the restaurant where they were seated.

"Don't you think it would be best, I mean as a mother, a *good* mother, to make sure your son is in a safe environment?"

"What do you know about my son? Who are you? Who sent you here?"

"No one sent me, but when you hear what I have to say, I think you'll agree with me that the best place for your sweet little boy is with his father, his biological father, that is."

The woman's eyebrows rose and her mouth fell open. "I'm not sitting here listening to you

57

anymore. You're crazy. You don't know a thing about me, my husband, my son or any of my children. I don't know who you are or what you want, but don't you *ever* contact me again!" The woman prepared to stand up from the table.

"Suit yourself...*Mariah.* I mean, what will happen when it comes out that your husband is an unregistered sex offender, and spent years behind bars for it. I'm sure you wouldn't want your circle of fake friends to know that. Oh, and I was just thinking, oh, my God, what would that mean for your son, Jude, poor little...what is he now...five...six years old? And he's there, under the same roof, with your perverted husband who is *not* even Jude's biological father? What will his *real* father have to say when he finds out his little boy is sleeping under the same roof with a pedophile that has a special fetish for little boys?"

"What is it you want?" The woman succumbed, and released an exasperated breath.

"Oh, don't you worry, I won't spare any details."

○

"I don't know why you're doing this," Mariah cried. "How could you, Hezekiah?"

"The question is how could *you*, Mariah? How could you marry a pedophile, and one who has a thing for boys? How could you live with a man like that and not know or turn a blind eye to his sick behavior?" Hezekiah's voice rumbled like thunder.

Mariah wiped the warm water flowing down her face with the back of her hand.

Hezekiah looked at Mariah without the least bit of pity. He was far too happy than to waste time thinking about her feelings. She hadn't thought about this all these years. He had six years to make up. Six years to really get to know his son.

And he had, of all people, Rianna to thank for this blessing.

"I can't believe you're doing this? How can you take my baby from me?" Mariah continued to cry, sitting outside Hezekiah's lawyer's office.

"Oh *stop*, it, Mariah. It's all about the money for you. You're just scared I'm going to stop paying child support. Well, you know what, Mariah? You're right. I am!" Hezekiah laughed loudly and obtrusively. "You'll be so lucky if I don't come after *you* for support. Now, go get my son," he demanded after Mariah reluctantly signed over temporary guardianship to Hezekiah.

epilogue

"Manipulation can give you anything in life you want, if you can afford it." M.F. Moonzajer

"I'm overcome with happiness. God is so good. You're so good," Hezekiah cried, lifting and twirling Rianna around and around in Apartment 3D while Jude played with his Star Wars Legos in the corner of her apartment.

"How did you do it? Tell me how you pulled this off?"

"I told you. I love you, Hezekiah. I'd do anything to prove that to you. Don't you see that now, baby?"

Hezekiah sat on the couch, rubbing his hand back and forth across his balding head.

"My baby boy, my son, Jude, is going to live with me. I...I can't believe it. I've got to get the house ready. Baby, I hope you know that I have to move into Lion's Gate. This seems like a dream. I can't believe it's real."

Rianna kissed him fully on the lips. She dismissed the continued lie Hezekiah told. He knew darn well he was already living in Lion's Gate, if only *he* knew that *she* knew. She remained silent about it now that she'd gotten Hezekiah's son from under his mother's roof. Sooner rather than later, she believed she would be moving into the house behind the gate as well!

"Don't worry," Rianna assured Hezekiah. "It's not a dream. It's all true." She looked over at the little boy. "He's living with you now. I mean, what else can she do? Like your lawyer advised, it was in her best interest, and her son's best interest, to let

60

things cool off until she can find out what they're going to do about her pedophile husband."

"Yeah, I...I just can't thank you enough. I owe you," Hezekiah cried, grabbing Rianna's face and kissing her deeply and passionately. "What can I do to ever repay you?"

Rianna smiled on the inside. *Let me count the ways....*

Words from the Author

Another story down and countless more to go for as long as the good Lord says so and gives me stories to write.

In "The Woman In Apartment 3D" we see again how jealousy can make a person do foolish things, and all in the so called "'name of love."

Some women (and men too) don't know when to say, *this is not for me and that I need to move on.* Many women and men in lifeless relationships don't want to admit *this is not the person God has for me, and I need to move on, trusting He will send me the person that is best for me.*

Yep, if it were only that simple. If we only followed that wise advice. Unfortunately most of the time, it's not like that. We allow jealousy and heartbreak to make us behave in unacceptable ways. We call it all in the name of love, but love should not act like a heathen. Love shouldn't make us act crazy, or hurt other people, or even kill people. Love is patient, kind, and not envious or puffed up. Let's learn to love and learn to forgive and move on.

On to the next story.....

Ruthless Rianna
Story 3

Additional titles by Shelia E. Bell
(Some titles may still be under former name Shelia Lipsey)

Young Adult Titles
House of Cars
The Life of Payne
The Lollipop Girl
The Righteous Brothers

Standalone Novels
Show A Little Love (*out of print*)
Always Now and Forever Love Hurts
Into Each Life
Sinsatiable
What's Blood Got To Do With It?
Only In My Dreams
The House Husband
Cross Road
Forever Ain't Enough

Series Books

Beautiful Ugly
True Beauty

My Son's Wife Series
My Son's Wife: The Beginning (Book 1)
My Son's Ex-Wife: Aftershock (Book 2)
My Son's Next Wife (Book 3)
My Sister My Momma My Wife (Book 4)
My Wife My Baby...And Him (Book 5)
The McCoy's of Holy Rock (Book 6)
Dem McCoy Boys (Book 7)
My Brother, Father...And Me (Book 8)
My Truth, My Time, My Turn (Book 9)
Dem Folk at Holy Rock (Book 10)
Thicker Than Water (Book 11)

Holy Rock Chronicles
Calling Dr. Daniels
The Woman in Apartment 3D

Ruthless Rianna

Adverse City Series
The Real Housewives of Adverse City
The Real Housewives of Adverse City 2
The Real Housewives of Adverse City 3
The Real Housewives of Adverse City 4

Anthologies
Bended Knees
Weary to Will
Learning to Love Me
Show A Little Love (1)

Nonfiction
A Christian's Perspective: Journey Through Grief
How to Live Your Life Like It's Golden

Follow me on Amazon bit.ly/sheliabell

Contact information
www.sheliaebell.net
www.sheliawritesbooks.com
sheliawritesbooks@yahoo.com
www.facebook.com/sheliawritesbooks
@sheliaebell (Twitter & Instagram)
@literacyrocks (Instagram)
@bwabclitfest (twitter)

Please join my mailing list for literary updates and
new book release information
www.sheliawritesbooks.com

If you enjoyed this book or any of my books, please
go to your favorite review site and leave a review!

Follow my Amazon Author Page bit.ly/sheliabell

Other links to my books

bit.ly/sheliaebell
bit.ly/sheliabn